# LARA CROFT TOMB RAIDER

# The Official Film Companion

In grateful memory of
Frederick S. Clarke (1949–2000), genius
editor of *Cinefantastique* magazine

THIS IS A CARLTON BOOK

Design copyright © 2001 Carlton Books Limited

This edition published by Carlton Books Limited 2001
20 Mortimer Street
London
W1N 7RD

A CIP catalogue for this book is
available from the British Library.

ISBN 1 84222 323 2

EXECUTIVE EDITOR: Sarah Larter
EDITOR: Mike Flynn
DESIGN: Adam Wright, Peter Bailey
PRODUCTION: Garry Lewis

Printed in Italy

# The Official Film Companion

## Alan Jones

Based on the motion picture written by
**Patrick Massett & John Zinman**
and **Simon West**

CARLTON
**BOOKS**

# CONTENTS

# FOREWORD

The most important thing to understand about the making of *Tomb Raider* is that everyone involved with the production was enamoured of Lara Croft. I mean, how could any of us not be after having played the game, or seen any of the hundreds of magazine covers she's graced or viewed one of her TV commercials. What is it about her? Well, speaking for myself, we live pretty dull lives compared to Lara. Archeologist, adventurer, explorer, ass-kicker. And yet, as exceptional and smart and wickedly humorous as she is, she's also infinitely relatable. You get the idea that there's something missing in her life, an emptiness in her heart that she's desperate to fill. What is she looking for? Some ancient relic or some kind of emotional and spiritual fulfillment?

So what the world has with Lara is an action hero for the twenty-first century: as accomplished and aspirational and cool as she is, she could probably use a good therapist as well. And with this new kind of action hero, we wanted to create a movie and a world around her that would reflect just how unique and different she was from the action heroes we had seen before her. She is the embodiment of modern and hi-tech cool and she has unlimited resources.

From wardrobe to production design to visual effects the same questions were asked over and over again. Does it reflect who Lara Croft is and represents? Is it consistent with being an heiress, an explorer, a rebel and the myriad of complicated elements of Lara's personality. Is it real? Is it cool? Would we kill to live in the world we are creating for Lara.

We also wanted to create a movie that was true to the game in the sense that Lara's adventures take her around the globe, which gave us the opportunity to embrace one of the great things about movies – to take an audience somewhere they've never been before. The production took us from London to Iceland and the stages of Pinewood Studios to Venice, and, most amazingly of all, the temples of Angkor Wat in Cambodia. And into this mix of real and historical worlds, we explored realms of fantasy and adventure which were influenced by ancient cultures, myths and philosophies.

*Tomb Raider* was a great adventure for all of us and I hope this book allows you to share the experience that we all had in the making of the movie, as well as shed some light on the production process itself and all of its extremely complicated logistics. I think the book also stands as a great testimony to the extraordinary and hard work of the many many talented people who worked on *Tomb Raider* , though you and I both know that they really had no choice: Lara Croft provided the inspiration herself.

**LLOYD LEVIN**

H

PART ONE:

# THE HISTORY OF LARA CROFT

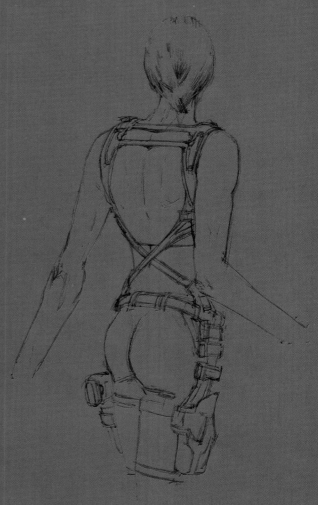

t all began with Laura Cruise. That was the name originally given to the main character of an innovative computer game, which in a short space of time, would become a landmark for the software industry, turn into one of the most consistent and best-selling game series of all time and establish a virtual goddess who would achieve unparalleled media status as a sexy, intelligent and take-charge icon for the digital age.

Founded by Jeremy Heath-Smith in 1988, the Derby, England-based Core Design Limited

(a fully owned subsidiary of the Eidos Interactive group since 1996) shot to the top of the United Kingdom computer games sales chart with *Rick Dangerous,* their first title in the rapidly expanding market place, and followed that achievement with the subsequent bestsellers *Chuck Rock, Thunderhawk, Darkmere, Battle Corps, Wonder Dog* and *Fighting Force*. But it wasn't until early 1995 that the Core Design team hit upon a brilliant concept that would propel them into the record books, make them world famous to legions of manic games players and score their most spectacular success.

"The idea was to create a computer game with the look of a movie," says Adrian Smith, the younger brother of Core Design's Managing Director, Jeremy, and Operations Director of the company. "During our brainstorming session we came up with the concept of a corridor-style game featuring a mix of exploration, action and puzzle-solving, played from a third person point of view. We knew it was important to create a central character people could relate to and imperative we put them in as real a world as possible. The character had to have complete freedom of movement to explore all areas of a state-of-the-art, highly-detailed interactive gaming environment."

With this basic concept approved, the project entered its first experimental stages. Level designers started researching and replicating possible locations using custom-built software and programmers began development of a brand new game engine. A scriptwriter was hired to produce a movie-style storyline and to give the game characters their identities. And artist Toby Gard began thinking seriously about the look and what compelling attributes the main character should embody. "Where the game should be located was a pretty easy decision to make once Egypt was mentioned," continues Smith. "We needed somewhere shrouded in mystery with hints of the mystical and, with its pyramids, exotic landscapes and archaeological history, Egypt clearly gave us a lot of scope to explore such colourful, suspenseful and exciting terrain."

At this crucial point the central character was being mooted as a male protagonist for no other reason than that was the game trend at the time. "But when we thought long and hard about it, we figured it was about time the

macho stereotype took a back seat," recalls Smith. "Plus we didn't want the new game to focus merely on shooting. Instead we wanted the character to be agile, athletic and someone who would captivate the player, engender sympathy and make them feel protective towards the danger they faced. In movies, the gun-toting, muscle-bound hero, as exemplified by Sylvester Stallone and Arnold Schwarzenegger, was clearly on the way out, and it became increasingly obvious to all of us formulating the new game that the main character just had to be female. That fulfilled all the initial requirements we had for the game while still retaining the elements of coy shyness and slight vulnerability we felt were important and cutting edge. Everyone told us

not to make her a woman and that we were absolutely crazy to do so but every element we wanted to encompass only pointed us more in that direction. Looking back I can hardly claim we had any real revolutionary attitude about what we were doing. Yet it just seemed so right to feature a feisty female and that was the line of development we doggedly continued to follow."

With Laura Cruise initially suggested as the name for the key character, the Core Design animators moved into action to create a whole series of graceful and fluid moves to denote the intelligence, resourcefulness and independence of what they envisioned as her strong and resilient personality. With statistics to rival those of Pamela Anderson, the physical

" Lara was clearly
the right character
at precisely the
right time ..."

ADRIAN SMITH, CORE DESIGN

strength to indulge in fearless acrobatic stunts and her assured proficiency with a pair of pistols, Toby Gard conceptualized Laura as a hot cyberbabe dressed in combat shorts, a turquoise tank top and Doc Marten boots. "However, we started thinking her name was too American," remarks Smith. "And, because we are a British-based company, we thought it proper to change her name and make her part of the English aristocracy. That would also give her the privileged lifestyle she would need to fund her adventurous and hazardous hobby."

So Lara Croft was born. Smith adds, "Lara, because it wasn't too far off our well-liked initial forename Laura, and Croft, because that countrified surname seemed to embody the very essence of 'Rule Britannia' Englishness. Once we had the complete Lara Croft character and psyche in our heads, she was immediately assigned her first adventure – *Tomb Raider.*"

As the mooted *Tomb Raider* plot developed along basic fantasy adventure thriller lines, so did Lara's passion for high-energy adventure and death-defying jeopardy as she raided sinister tombs and discovered priceless artifacts and treasures in the secret, booby-trapped burial chambers of dingy pyramids. Full-motion video sequences portrayed her as an inquisitive,

daring and intrepid international explorer who would literally stop at nothing to achieve her goals. First unveiled to the public in May 1996 at the American trade show E3, the game attracted exceptionally high levels of interest as never before had such a versatile and powerful female character been featured in a computer game. Launched in November 1996, *Tomb Raider* entered the sales charts at Number One and Lara's continuing adventures through *Tomb Raider II, Tomb Raider III, Tomb Raider: The Last Revelation* and *Tomb Raider: Chronicles* have continued to break records. *Tomb Raider II* became the fastest-selling title in the computer games industry's history and to date the combined *Tomb Raider* series has sold well over thirty million units worldwide and won a host of awards, most notably a BAFTA for outstanding contribution to the industry.

Yet while the games themselves attracted outstanding reviews in every specialist publication and acclaim from sleepy-eyed players, sustained media interest began to escalate thanks to what everyone considered the most important component of the game – Lara Croft herself. Smith points out, "Initially, *Tomb Raider* was our prime focus, but suddenly Lara became the hot news item. People kept asking us questions about her past, when her birthday was and other personal things like that. Soon we found we had to create a proper well-rounded character to keep up with all the demands from her increasing fan base." Due to such widespread fanatical interest, Lara Croft became firmly established as a major star in her own right. Offers flooded in for licensing deals and product endorsements, the rock group U2 requested footage of their virtual heroine in action to be played on their Jumbotron video screen during their PopMart world tour in 1997 and the British Minister for Science, Lord Sainsbury, even named Lara an Ambassador for British Scientific Excellence.

It was the trend-setting British lifestyle magazine *The Face* that turned Lara Croft into the

**Opposite, Top**: Lara and her trusted ally Bryce. **Opposite, Bottom**: Lara Croft, Tomb Raider. **Above**: Lara executes a "bungee ballet" above the high-tech interior of Croft Manor.

first true supermodel of the cyber age. In June 1997 the magazine published an extensive and unprecedented feature on the character's sensational rise in popularity and what it meant in pop culture terms. It was also the first time a non-human celebrity had featured on the magazine's cover and been allowed to interrupt the masthead. Since that accolade, Lara Croft has continued to demand unprecedented media coverage worldwide. Articles in *Time*, *Newsweek* and *Rolling Stone* have documented the Croft phenomenon, Lara has appeared in both rock videos and television commercials and an official range of merchandise has produced a wide range of clothing and accessories.

Such overwhelming press and public attention caused even more interest in Lara Croft and forced Core Design to construct a biography to answer the most widely asked questions. The biography has been modified for the film, which sees Lara as the daughter of famed archaeologist Lord Henshingly Croft. Brought up in the secure world of the British aristocracy at her ancestral home in Surrey, tragedy struck early in her life when her father mysteriously disappeared while on a remote expedition. Deeply saddened by his absence, it was when Lara moved from Wimbledon High School to Gordonstoun that she began to take an interest in her father's work. The nearby Scottish Highlands also became an ideal place for her to explore and train as she became increasingly obsessed with discovering ancient artifacts and forgotten civilizations. After completing her education at a Swiss finishing school, it was the return trip from a vacation in the Himalayas that was to seal Lara's career fate as her plane crashed in the mountains and she was the sole survivor.

Escaping from this adversity was a harrowing experience, yet it became the defining moment of her life because she only felt truly alive when faced with such hazardous dangers. From this point on, Lara rejected the suffocating atmosphere of upper class British society to travel alone, searching the far corners of the world for priceless art and other unusual antiques. To fund her adventures, rather than pillage the remnants of the past for profit, Lara worked as a photojournalist and won a number of Pulitzer prizes for her contribution to the art. For Lara, tomb raiding is a way of life, not a profession, and that's why she forged such a high profile name for herself in the field.

Adrian Smith is still amazed at Lara's overnight fame. "Lara was clearly the right character at precisely the right time. Featuring a lead woman shook up the die-hard male game-players and also caused *Tomb Raider* to cross over into the female market. I also think she got caught up in the whole Girl Power vibe that was prevalent at the time thanks to the Spice Girls. But I don't think it's just one single thing that has made Lara one of the most instantly recognizable figures of the past decade. People seem to relate to Lara's dynamic appeal and positive attitude and aspire to be like her. They also love the mystery that surrounds her action-packed lifestyle – where she's really coming from and the whole mystique about her background. I do think the *Tomb Raider* series also opened up the possibilities of what people now expect from a computer game. They wanted an escapist experience like the movie-going one and they got it in spades. Because we always visualized *Tomb Raider* in cinematic terms, licensing a movie version of the game seemed exactly right as the next logical step in her format progression. Never in our wildest dreams could we have predicted the nuclear explosion we were creating with Lara Croft. It still staggers me and I know that feeling – a mixture of pride and amazement – will surface again when I see the *Tomb Raider* movie in all its glory for the first time."

## "For Lara tomb raiding is a way of life ..."

# 2

# THE GENESIS OF TOMB RAIDER THE MOVIE

A s the original *Tomb Raider* game became an international sales phenomenon, and the central Lara Croft character invaded public consciousness to such an extent that her meteoric rise to global fame was assured, Core Design found their creation inevitably fuelling interest in Hollywood circles. "It was around the time of the launch of the *Tomb Raider II* game when there was talk about a movie possibility and the Hollywood film industry came knocking on our doors," explains Core Design's Adrian Smith. "The first offer we received came from a famous animation studio but we really didn't think it was the right route to pursue. That wouldn't have signalled too much of a quantum leap from the game itself. However, the offer made us realize the potential and merit of granting a movie license to the right studio. We just had to make sure we weighed up all the pros and cons before we chose the people to work with. Uppermost in all our minds was the fear of putting the creative essence of *Tomb Raider* in someone else's hands. The less control you have over something can be disconcerting so we knew it was vital to pick the right studio to nurture the concept and Lara's image. There was no way we were going to let our property end up on movie screens looking like *Super Mario Bros.*, *Mortal Kombat* or *Streetfighter*! So, when other Hollywood movie offers flooded in, we were careful to look at each very closely indeed."

One of the many proposals Eidos received came from Paramount Pictures, courtesy of veteran independent Hollywood producer Lawrence Gordon and his business partner Lloyd Levin. The prolific and highly regarded Gordon had produced numerous blockbuster hits, including *Die Hard*, *Predator*, *Field Of Dreams* and *48 Hours*, while Levin had produced *Boogie Nights*, *The Rocketeer* and *Event Horizon*.

"I was very familiar with the *Tomb Raider* game as I played it a lot and had a real respect and affinity for it," says Levin. "We pursued the movie rights because it had a real character at its centre and the game storylines were very cinematic in approach. To our minds, the *Tomb Raider* ethos offered something that hadn't been seen in movies before. It had exotic adventure, thrilling action, treasure hunts and mortal danger – all given a very

**ABOVE:** Angelina Jolie and director Simon West on the set of *Tomb Raider*.

modern spin with a unique character at the foreground embodying the spirit of contemporary cool."

Levin continues, "I'm convinced we ultimately acquired the licence in 1997 mainly because we told Eidos and the Core Design team stuff they didn't want to hear. Other studios seemed to be offering them everything in the world to secure the rights: yes, we will put the movie into production immediately; yes, it will be out this time next year. Well, we went in and said we wanted to take it very slowly and assured them we wouldn't disrupt the mythology they had worked so hard to build up. We told them we wanted to extend their brainchild in terms of Lara's personal life and the kind of inner stories she could be involved in. We also wanted to keep a close collaborative relationship going with Core because we knew there would be a lot of inevitable frustration along the way.

Every project takes time to develop and such setbacks come with the territory. Yet we guaranteed that no matter how long it would take to get the property exactly right we would always remain committed and enthusiastic. We were in the frame because we wanted to look after Lara and do the right things with her – not because she was simply the latest hot property to pursue."

Every salient point Gordon and Levin remarked upon struck a chord with Core Design. As Smith explains, "We knew nothing about the film business because it's a whole different ball game to our industry, but we chose the Paramount deal because Larry and Lloyd basically said, 'Look, this is a property you've owned for five years, built up and made successful and we want to continue that upward curve'. That was such a refreshing approach for us and it was one that made us feel safe rather than anxiously protective. They clearly understood the property and knew how passionate we were about it. Actually, I warmed to Lloyd instantly the first time we met because he kept asking for tips about the game he was stuck on! "

"If we didn't like anything about the script, the casting or the general direction the project was going in, all we had to do was say so and they assured us they would change it. And they were true to their word in every respect. From a very early stage we felt comfortable with Paramount and every artistic decision they were making."

For Levin, the relationship with Eidos and Core Design couldn't have been more mutually beneficial. He adds, "From the moment we signed the contract, we had nothing but cooperation on their part. There were a few contractual vetoes. For example, Lara was not allowed to smoke, use bad language or have any frontal nudity, but we wouldn't have wanted such scenes included anyway as the movie was always going to be aimed at the family audience. It was never a question of Core saying, no, you can't do this or that, it was always a case of us approaching them with our ideas for open discussions. Frankly, I thought they would

be more disapproving over certain aspects, but more often than not they were always genuinely excited over what we brought to the table. One of the key changes we wanted to make in the film concerned Lara's outfit. We thought long and hard about whether to clothe Lara in her trademark brown shorts, turquoise top and boots or not, but we eventually decided that a wardrobe change was the right decision now the character was entering a different medium. We were nervous about broaching the subject with Core as we had no idea how it would fly with them. However, they had decided to change Lara's costumes for the new game they were working on at the time anyway [*Tomb Raider: The Last Revelation*] and what they had envisaged was remarkably similar to our own designs. So a certain amount of synergy seemed to be working in our favour too."

Once Gordon and Levin had secured the *Tomb Raider* movie rights, they started developing scripts that would rise to the potential of the basic concept and boldly encompass Lara's heritage rather than merely exploit it. "It was

**LEFT**: Lara and Wilson (Leslie Phillips) try to solve the puzzle of the mysterious clock found at Croft Manor.

a tall order," points out Levin. "The important thing was to constantly pursue the levels of excellence the games had achieved and not allow it to become reminiscent or derivative of anything seen before. None of us could get lazy about our combined efforts to take new directions in terms of never-before-seen adventure landscapes, character dynamics and emotional arcs. In this endeavour Core Design became a tremendous resource for us as they knew everything about Lara's universe and what would be correct or incorrect about the avenues we were pursuing. It was fantastic to have people at our disposal who could instantly answer questions and supply all the necessary information we needed about even the smallest detail."

Although various draft screenplays of *Tomb Raider* were written under various titles, including *Tomb Raider: The Achilles Shield* and *Tomb Raider: The Adventures of Lara Croft*, the whole project didn't properly snap into sharp focus until Simon West came on board as the director. British-born West began his award-winning career in 1981 as a trainee editor with BBC television in London and, after winning a grant from the Arts Council to write and direct the film *Dolly Mixtures*, he joined Limelight, one of the fastest growing pop video and commercials production companies in the British capital. After winning the Best Video Award for Mel and Kim's chart hit "Respectable" at the Montreux Music Festival, he moved to Los Angeles and directed a string of successful commercials. Soon Hollywood studios beckoned and West joined the mainstream film industry in 1997 with the all-action blockbuster *Con Air*, starring Nicolas Cage and John Malkovich. Two years later he directed the big budget thriller *The General's Daughter*, starring John Travolta.

"I was looking for my next project after wrapping *The General's Daughter*," says West, "and I was determined to direct something completely opposite to the dark claustrophobic tone of that picture. I wanted fun, fantasy and imagination so I could exercise all the other muscles I hadn't used in my movie work so far. I'd heard about the *Tomb Raider* project on the Hollywood network – as you do – but I turned it down twice because I had my own definite ideas about what angles should be explored with it. I can't honestly say I was a fan of the game as I never have much time to play it. But when I did play *Tomb Raider*, I thought it was intelligent, creative, enormous fun and obviously streets ahead of its rivals. Then, around Christmas time 1999, I was offered the chance to direct the project again. I thought about it more seriously this time: hmmm, this could be very cool, and Lara Croft was such an appealing character. So I decided to read the latest commissioned script but didn't like it. It was just what you'd expect – *Raiders of the Lost Ark* with a woman instead of Harrison Ford. Plus, it had a very clichéd view of England that put it squarely in the *Austin Powers* bracket – you know – tea with the Queen at Buckingham Palace, red buses and 'bobbies' on the beat. I told Larry Gordon and Lloyd Levin that I would only direct *Tomb Raider* if I could keep the title and Lara but change everything else in the script and start from scratch. I added that it was a unique opportunity to develop Lara's personality and bring her to a wider audience while putting an excitingly fresh spin on the entire fantasy adventure genre. They agreed and I officially came on board."

Lloyd Levin remarks, "Unlike the other directors on our consideration shortlist, Simon was the one who took the whole idea completely to heart. He had a rich conception of what the story could be, not only from the scale and fun points of view but also on the sub-textual levels. We always knew the trap would be to end up

"I thought ... hmmm, this could be very cool, and Lara Croft was such an appealing character."

SIMON WEST, DIRECTOR

making another Indiana Jones-style adventure but Simon embraced everything about *Tomb Raider* that was unique and had never been seen on screen before. He had a specific story to tell, one he felt was important to accomplish with the Lara Croft character. Simon was also British and instinctively knew how not to fall into a tourist view of the culture. He had a born perspective on what it meant to be aristocracy, complete with the class sensibilities and nuances. We were convinced he could inform the *Tomb Raider* reality in a way that would be worth capturing for maximum entertainment value. It wasn't a hard decision to make on our part to let him have carte blanche with the story."

Simon West's arrival on the scene was welcome news to everyone on the gaming side, says Adrian Smith. "When we heard about Simon's involvement we all heaved a huge sigh of relief. None of us were particularly impressed by any of the draft screenplays submitted to us for our approval. Although it had been an early suggestion, none of us at Core Design tried to come up with our own story despite the fact we had every single Lara Croft back-story memorized. Simon simply went through the script like a dose of salts and that was very reassuring. We figured this guy knew what he was doing – his past successes in the field spoke volumes for his talent and expertise – and, as he wasn't trying to tell us about our business, we certainly weren't going to tell him about his."

The director immersed himself in mountains of research to get the *Tomb Raider* story pitch perfect. He explains, "I got Core Design to send over everything on the game and Lara, and I scanned through every magazine relating to archaeological subject matter I could find, from *New Scientist* to *National Geographic*. I looked at classic quest movies and big epics, like *Dr Zhivago* and *Lawrence of Arabia*, watched every documentary on ancient civilizations and read every book on mysticism, sacred geometry, alchemic artifacts, religious rites, astrology and planet alignment theories. The story evolved from all these strands."

The epic tale revolves around a secret organization, called the *Illuminati*, who are searching for an ancient clock that is the key to opening both time and space. With the clock as their guide, the *Illuminati* need to find two halves of a mystical triangle, made from crystallized meteor metal, used five thousand years ago to vanquish their sworn enemies. If the two pieces are ever combined again, time will stop and the fate of mankind will be changed forever.

When Lara Croft finds the clock hidden in Croft Manor – her late father Lord Croft acquired the priceless icon during one of his many archaeological digs – it fuels her adventurous streak and sets her on the most dangerous and high stakes quest of her entire exploring career. With just forty-eight hours before all the planets align for a total eclipse – when the sacred triangle's power will be at it most potent – Lara must stop Manfred Powell, the *Illuminati*'s evil emissary, finding the two halves first and joining them together. The death-defying mission takes her initially to Cambodia, where the Tomb of the Dancing Light holds one half of the puzzle, and then to Siberia, where the Tomb of

that immediately gave me the advantage of using all the new technologies available. The central themes are the sort of New Age and mystical, phenomena we don't properly understand, rather than have Lara just fighting nasty Nazis. It was an exciting challenge reinventing the 'Event Movie' genre for an expectant audience comprising of people who know nothing

## "In many ways I envisioned Lara Croft as a female James Bond for the new millennium."

### SIMON WEST – DIRECTOR

Ten Thousand Shadows hides the other. With her trusty computer-savvy sidekick Bryce, Lara takes on Powell, his assistant Mr Pimms and mercenary archaeologist Alex West (Lara's occasional accomplice) to save the Universe from prophesied disaster.

"There was a conscious effort to distance the story as far from the Indiana Jones trilogy as possible on all levels," points out West. "That's why I stayed away from sand, snakes, pyramids, rats, bugs or anything yellow. There was no way I was going to spend a year of my life working in an environment I'd seen a hundred times already and one that's been copied and pastiched to death. Luckily, the *Tomb Raider* game was set in modern times so it wasn't going to be a thirties period piece anyway, and

about the game and ardent game-players themselves."

West adds, "I figured the last thing gamers would want to see is what they've already played for nine hours – with better lighting and in three dimensions! They will be well satisfied with the finished result because they get to know more details about Lara, how she speaks – above the little noises she makes when bumping into things – and what the rest of Croft Manor actually looks like. I mean, what does someone who's gorgeous, loaded and a famous explorer do to relax and what does she keep in her basement? All those questions and many more get fun and inventive answers during the course of the turbo-driven action. But I didn't think it would be fair to ignore the game players totally

and not take them into account. So, for them, I've woven into the screenplay lots of little coded messages and intriguing puzzles that they will be able to unpick and decipher and, if they are very clever, be able to work out what's going on long before the rest of the audience."

"In many ways I envisioned Lara Croft as a female James Bond for the new millennium," continues West. "Everyone wants to be like her, or have her as their girlfriend. But we were not constrained like Bond and that's what appealed to me the most. It was a totally open brief. Nor was I constrained by reality, although I did set certain rules for the movie. When you're above ground, everything is pretty much plausible. I push it now and again as there are weird phenomena in the world we can't explain. But when the characters go underground, into the tombs, I changed those rules completely. The gloves are off and almost anything can happen. There's a very purposeful surreal element *to Tomb Raider* that still makes sense in the overall scheme of things."

PART THREE:

# LARA CROFT AND ANGELINA JOLIE

reporting that Sandra (*While You Were Sleeping*) Bullock, Sporty Spice, Denise (*The World Is Not Enough*) Richards and model Anna Nicole Smith were allegedly under consideration. However, the truth of the matter was that West only ever wanted one star to play Lara. And that star was Angelina Jolie.

West explains, "Angelina was always my only choice. It was a one-horse race. If she didn't do it, I couldn't think of anyone else who would be suitable. All of Angelina's performances to date have been a heady combination of gorgeously voluptuous womanhood but with brains, wit and good humour. Those were precisely the attributes Lara had to have and Angelina completely embodied them. We all agreed Lara had to be more than an action cartoon cut-out as her character had many emotional and heartfelt scenes to tackle. Therefore we not only needed a stunning looking woman but also a great actress who could pull such scenes off in a totally believable fashion. I firmly believed only Angelina would be able to act her way out of tight dramatic corners while never losing Lara's sexual appeal or winning qualities. I also instinctively knew Angelina would satisfy the demands of the games fans and their preconceived ideas of what Lara looked like. It was an opinion shared by the producers and Eidos and I was ecstatic when Angelina accepted the challenge."

Once director Simon West had agreed to take on *Tomb Raider* attention turned to finding the right actress to play the all-important central role of Lara Croft. Although model/actresses Rhona Mitra, Nell McAndrew, Lara Weller and Lucy Clarkson had all appeared in costume as Lara at trade shows for promotional purposes, many casting rumours appeared in the media and on the internet

Born in Los Angeles on June 4, 1975, the daughter of Oscar-winning actor Jon Voight and Marcheline Betrand, Angelina Jolie (her middle name) harboured childhood dreams of becoming a funeral director. She once explained that startling career option by revealing, "I'm not famous Lee Strasberg Theatre Institute before working as a professional model in the fashion capitals of the world.

After appearing in rock videos for Meat Loaf, Lenny Kravitz and The Lemonheads, she acted in five student films for the University of

obsessed by death. The truth is I'm probably the least morbid person one could meet. But if I think about death more than some other people, it is probably because I love life more than they do." Happily, for her future admirers, Angelina jettisoned that occupation and instead, after majoring in film at New York University, trained and performed at the Southern California School of Cinema, all directed by her brother, James Haven, before making her first major foray into screen acting with *Cyborg 2: Glass Shadow* (1993). Learning her craft through such movies as *Hackers* (1995) – the first time she worked in Britain and where she met her first husband, co-star Jonny Lee Miller – *Love Is All There Is* (1996),

*Foxfire* (1996) and *Playing God* (1997), it was her moving and sensitive performances in two television movies that made Hollywood sit up and take notice. Playing Cornelia Wallace in *George Wallace* (1997) and the AIDS-stricken model Gia Carangi in *Gia* (1998) won her wide

won the Best Supporting Actress Oscar for her role as the troubled mental patient Lisa Rowe in *Girl, Interrupted* (1999) and was recently named by *People* magazine as one of the fifty most beautiful people in the world.

"Playing Lara Croft is the hardest job I've

> ## "Angelina was always my only choice. It was a one-horse race. If she didn't do it, I couldn't think of anyone else who would be suitable."
>
> ### SIMON WEST, DIRECTOR

acclaim, two Golden Globe Awards and an Emmy Award nomination for the latter.

Angelina's career rise has been meteoric ever since, with the high profile movies *Playing By Heart* (1998), *Pushing Tin* (1999) – where she met her second husband, co-star Billy Bob Thornton – *The Bone Collector* (1999), *Gone In 60 Seconds* (2000) and *Original Sin* (2001). She

ever done," admits Angelina. "She's not moody, brooding or so wrapped up in herself like a lot of the other characters I've tackled before. Lara is very clear about herself and her goals and overly capable in an almost beyond-human way. I certainly don't feel like that when I wake up every morning, so I've often had to snap myself into Lara mode in order to

take on the world like she does every single day. It's so hard to stay in a positive, healthy, clear and brave state of mind all the time. It's much easier to internalize and remain dark, which is what I've been used to playing up until now. The strange thing is, when I accepted the Lara part, I thought it was going to be a major departure from everything else I've done in the past. Okay, it's a blockbuster fantasy and I've never done one of those before, but the essence of Lara has turned out to be remarkably similar to some other roles I've played. She's alone, focused on justice, is a little crazy in many ways, bold (definitely), loves her freedom and is very sexual. Those are traits I adore in people in general and the themes I've explored in movies before. Lara is the perfect woman in my estimation."

## "Lara is the perfect woman in my estimation."

There is an apocryphal story that Angelina accepted the Lara Croft part to annoy her first husband, Jonny Lee Miller, as he would continually ignore her to keep playing the *Tomb Raider* game. "I do keep reading the most bizarre things about myself in the media and that story is just one of them," she laughs. "It is true that Jonny played the game non-stop and I ended up hating Lara because she was the one keeping him up all night and not me!

But getting revenge on Jonny certainly wasn't the reason why I took on the role. Billy Bob's children play the game too and I have tried to beat them at it but I kill Lara constantly. Playing the quintessential video game pin-up was a major challenge and making her human has been my biggest contribution to *Tomb Raider*. We have altered her a bit for the movie. My Lara has still got what makes her a cyber icon, but I'm more athletic rather than curvy, in control rather than cute. She's built in a certain way and I've adjusted that to make her stronger both physically and mentally. I'm all for curves and sexiness in a woman, and there was no way I was going to hide from that, yet I feel I've made her a three-dimensional female in every aspect."

She continues, "I think of Lara in terms of being a tomboy who accents her feminine side without even realizing it. The one quality I like about her above everything else is that there's a certain strength in being a woman and she enjoys that without submerging it in misplaced bravado. She faces incredible dangers yet she's never overwhelmed by any of them. And that, to me, is what's different between Lara and any other action hero or heroine you can name. She's tremendously excited by all her adventures because it's her thing. Yet she never loses her sense of being a woman and nor does she hate men. I see Lara like a creature, an insane wild animal firing on every cylinder

"On one hand Lara is like an amalgam of every sexy Italian actress I've ever watched – Claudia Cardinale, Sophia Loren, Gina Lollobrigida – and on the other she's dog-sledding on top of a mountain in Siberia and laughing at the danger. Who needs therapy? The roles I choose are my therapy."

all of the time. I picture her as a cross between Sigourney Weaver (in *Alien*) and Crocodile Dundee! On one hand Lara is like an amalgam of every sexy Italian actress I've ever watched – Claudia Cardinale, Sophia Loren, Gina Lollobrigida – and on the other she's dog-sledding on top of a mountain in Siberia and laughing at the danger. Who needs therapy? The roles I choose are my therapy."

When Angelina agreed to play Lara Croft, she knew she would have to face three extreme challenges that she had never wrestled with before in her illustrious career. One was learning a British accent. "That part still makes me nervous as I won't know if I've totally succeeded until the film is released," she remarks. "I wanted Lara to sound like she had been raised with a certain breeding as Lady Croft, but I didn't want her to become an unapproachable and snobby aristocrat. I had to take pieces of that upper-class accent and make it more friendly and inviting. Sure, Lara is a perfect lady, but that comes with a violent edge thanks to her lifestyle. It was a fine balance and observing my British co-stars speaking was an enormous help."

The second learning curve area concerned all the stunt work Angelina had to be involved with. In the course of the *Tomb Raider* action, aside from her standard fighting skills, Lara battles a hulking android programmed with a CD-ROM mix of her favourite clashes from the past, does a bungee ballet through the great hall at Croft Manor, rides her Norton motorbike over a basement full of expensive collectible cars, balances on a descending log in the Tomb of the Dancing Light as it swings toward a huge booby-trapped Buddha idol, and jumps around a giant, moving metallic model of the Solar System in the Tomb of Ten Thousand Shadows.

She says, "I wanted to do as many of my own stunts as possible and stunt co-ordinator Simon Crane really put me through my paces with his fitness regime. For three months prior to the start of principal shooting (and during the *Gone In 60 Seconds* promotional junket) I gym-trained, worked out, ran for miles, rode bikes and cars, hit punch bags, went canoeing and somersaulted every other day. I was also put on a high protein diet to ensure maximum energy. The menu involved a disgusting amount of sardines and meat, but no caffeine. Simon Crane was an absolutely brilliant teacher because every action sequence was designed in exact relation to what I had trained for. The only skill I learnt that we didn't properly use was scuba diving. I got my diving licence during filming but the underwater scene I was preparing for eventually got cut from the script. Simon Crane had planned this huge underwater fight with hundreds of eels swimming around me but that was adjusted to five henchmen and a couple of eels. If Simon Crane had been in charge we'd have been filming for three years to get everything exactly right and include every stunt he planned for! He's the boldest stunt person I've ever met and, because he knew I'd try anything once, we've achieved amazing results".

The third leap of faith for Angelina came in the special effects department. Many of the cutting edge visual effects would be created digitally after the shooting event by supervisor Steve Begg with Mill Film and the Really Useful Companies. All the special, physical and mechanical effects, like the bungee ballet, swinging log and the moving Solar System, were achieved by veteran James Bond movie supervisor Chris Corbould actually on the array of stunning sets at Pinewood Studios in London. An example of the former is when Lara battles reanimated stone monkey warriors and six-armed swordsmen in the Tomb of the Dancing Light.

"You never get used to the fact that you're fighting a flying monkey, whether it's real or will be added later," laughs Angelina. "I was truly shocked by the mean look of the monkeys because I had pictured them like the ones in *The Wizard of Oz*. When I saw them on set looking so ugly and nasty, I wanted to go home! Yet facing such weirdness is part of Lara's appeal. It's almost like she looks at the audience, intimates she doesn't quite believe it either, but gets on with the job of fighting whatever because that's what she does. When explosions go off, they really do and that's quite hard to

deal with when you're surrounded by them. But it's the bungee ballet that proved the scariest effect of all from my point of view. At one point I was hanging off a wall and nearly dropped forty feet to the floor. Let me tell you, the look of terror you see captured on my face is very authentic. I really was panic-stricken."

Director Simon West may have only wanted Angelina as his *Tomb Raider* star, but the actress herself didn't commit to the project until she had actually met him and sounded him out. She explained, "I initially thought the whole idea of Simon wanting someone like me was a strange one. I mean, what had he seen in my past work that convinced him I was Lara Croft? As it represented a quantum leap into a whole new genre, I had to make sure I felt comfortable with Simon and that he was the right director to guide my performance. Well, we met, and he told me exactly how he saw Lara. He explained all about the magical elements, based on real myths, legends and cultures, he brought into the film, and why he wanted them there. He fired my imagination with ideas that went so far beyond anything I had conjured up myself. It amazed me, and still does, that his two prior films had such a masculine slant as I could see he was a director who really understood women. Once he described Lara as a warrior in a macho world, I was completely sold on the project."

Angelina's main worries about appearing in *Tomb Raider* concerned the fact that she would have to sign a two-sequel contract and that she would also be the eye of a franchise storm, complete with action toys based on her likeness. She remarks, "I wasn't sure I wanted someone snapping a hundred photos of me from all angles while I was in the middle of doing a complicated acting scene just so Lara's sunglasses would conform to the toy designs. I became an actress because I like to hide behind the characters I play. Despite the public's perception of me, I am a very private person who has a hard time with the fame thing, not that I care what people say about me. Did I really want to star in a massive blockbuster that was going to up my profile like never before and one that would make it impossible to disappear from the public eye? Would *Tomb Raider* make it difficult for producers to approach me with other offers after making such a different film from my norm? The opposite side to that was having some game players visit the set and see how thrilled and happy they were at everything they saw being done with their favourite character. They lived in Lara's world too and I was overjoyed to be able to answer all the questions they threw at

me while autographing their posters. That's what turned my whole attitude to the film around. I was the person these fans adored. It's my job as an actor to try and successfully become someone else and I'd achieved that with these visitors. Suddenly I felt good about what I was doing and all the nagging doubts about sequels – my face on the side of buses and action figures – vanished."

Angelina's impressive roster of *Tomb Raider* co-stars includes Iain Glen, Daniel Craig, Noah Taylor, Chris Barrie, Leslie Phillips, Richard Johnson and her own father, Jon Voight, who appears throughout Lara's quest in mono-chrome flashbacks offering advice, clues and support. She smiles, "When I read the script, and read all about Lara's special closeness to her late father, Lord Croft, I got really emotional because it reminded me so much of my own relationship with my father. He was such perfect casting that it was a bit scary. At first, I wasn't sure if he was the right choice but it soon became obvious that I wasn't going to feel right about anybody else doing it. As an actor in a script context I have always loved sharing everything about my personal feelings and to suddenly share something private about our own relationship was very special. The first scene we did together I don't think I've ever been so still in one particular moment. We were looking deep into each other's eyes and the words we spoke rang with a magical honesty.

I have always known that Jon loved me. Sometimes you never get the chance to tell people in your life how much you care about them. We really made a point of saying what we have always wanted to say to each other personally within the milieu of the film and it was so special."

She continues, "Lara and Lord Croft, Jon and me ... we share similar loves, ideas and a sense of adventure. Lara is curious about life, the past and her relationship with her father. Although she has the independence to figure things out for herself, her father is always there with little messages to point her in the right direction. Jon has always shared his wisdom with me, what life lessons he has learnt along the way, and constantly guided me. I've always admired him and felt I was a lot like him. I'm very proud of that and pleased we could both put those feelings across in *Tomb Raider*. How many people ever get to act with their father? It's the greatest thing in the world – even with our British accents! I can't remember if we've ever thought about making a film together before, as we are both on very specific, individual journeys. Yet how often does a script come along offering such a unique opportunity and

for the Tomb of the Dancing Light and *Tomb Raider* was the first film since *Lord Jim*, in 1964, to be allowed into that war torn, Far Eastern country.

She says, "Cambodia is the most amazing place I've ever been to in my life. I can honestly say that it changed my life and made me feel differently about everything – my life and my work. Just coming to Angkor Wat is the cherry on the whole *Tomb Raider* experience. For one scene I was under this beautiful waterfall with the most incredible jungle around me and I was overwhelmed to the point where I couldn't speak. For eight months we had all been making this movie together at a frantic pace, running and jumping around. Suddenly we got to Angkor Wat and everyone in the crew seemed to quieten down, get really happy, calm and friendly. The country does seem to have a magical quality that caused us all to bond together in a way he hadn't before. I don't think anyone in the crew who went to Cambodia will ever forget it. I know there are some people who think that we shouldn't have shot in such a special, spiritual place. At the same time, that's the wonderful thing about making a film and taking it out of a Hollywood context. To be able to tell a great story and share this stunning place with the rest of the movie-going world is just a brilliant thing to do."

She continues, "I want audiences to leave *Tomb Raider* wanting to explore other places

one mirroring our own thoughts and feelings? Rarely, and that's why we just had to do it."

If working with her father was a fantastic experience for Angelina, a close second was shooting on location in Cambodia. The fabled temple at Angkor Wat provided the exteriors in the world, like Cambodia. That's what it has made me want to do. It has made me excited about the sights in the world I haven't yet seen and the places I must get around to going to. Life can be really mundane and we all get wrapped up in the small details that don't matter much in the overall scheme of things. Go out and get on a plane and go somewhere you've never been to before. Go backpacking and meet people from different cultures. We all forget that sometimes and it's important not to do so. Deciding to star in *Tomb Raider* was along similar lines for me. I took the chance. Everyone is in danger of taking themselves far

too seriously in life and not doing what they want to because they're afraid people won't accept them. I don't really care what people are going to say about me as an actress after *Tomb Raider*. I know how hard and exhausting it was for me to make Lara Croft a great role model, but all the audience has to do is sit

back, have fun and enjoy her thrilling adventures. So have your own. You won't regret it. I certainly don't."

**4**

PART FOUR:

# ALLIES
# AND
# ENEMIES

" We're soul mates Lara.
We're living on the razor's
edge, you and me. We're in
it for the thrill, the money,
the buzz, the danger ..."

ALEX WEST TO LARA CROFT

## IAIN GLEN IS MANFRED POWELL

Lara Croft's main adversary in *Tomb Raider* is Manfred Powell. One of the most powerful members of the sinister *Illuminati* – the People of the Light – the cool, elegant and ruthless Powell clashed in the past with Lara's late father, Lord Croft, and will now do anything to possess the enchanted clock that leads to the locations of the two vital triangle pieces hidden in time and space.

Manfred Powell is played by Iain Glen, a gifted stage and screen actor whose films include *Gorillas In The Mist*, *Mountains of the Moon*, *Silent Scream* and *Fools of Fortune*. In recent years the Scottish actor, who trained at London's prestigious Royal Academy of Dramatic Art (RADA), has starred in the musical *Martin Guerre*, and made headlines across the world when he appeared as Nicole Kidman's leading man of choice in the controversial Donmar Warehouse stage production of *The Blue Room* in London and New York. The very first scene in *Tomb Raider* opens with Manfred Powell attending an *Illuminati* meeting in Venice.

Glen sets the scene: "Basically, I walk into this huge hall housing the *Illuminati* offices and the main man, the Distinguished Gentleman (played by veteran actor Richard Johnson), says, 'Our time has come'. We are desperate to capture this mysterious God-like power that only comes along every five thousand years with a certain planetary alignment. I more or less say, 'Trust me, I know exactly what I'm doing and everything is under control'. The truth is I haven't got a clue where to start looking for the clock, but that's Powell in a nutshell. He has such conviction, such inner belief in himself that he can busk the lies he's telling with finesse and wit. Isn't that the mark of all good villains?"

Glen landed the role in the standard way. "I got a telephone call from my agent who told me about the film and set up a meeting with director Simon West," he says. "It was a simple reading that was over in ten minutes. I did meet producer Lloyd Levin, who was very complimentary over my work in *The Blue Room*, so I guessed that's what made them think of me for the Powell part. I take all such readings with a pinch of salt in honesty. You have to remain philosophical as there are so many variables and additional elements as to whether something might work or not, so I promptly forgot about it. Ten days later they asked me to screen test and then it all happened fairly swiftly and sweetly. I tested with Angelina Jolie, we chopped and changed a few things in the audition scene and I was surprised at how much I enjoyed what is usually a groan-inducing chore. It was my first inkling of how much of a treat Angelina was to work with. She was generous, kind, warm and honest – and carried it off with such grace and good spirit – which is all you want from other actors. I knew then I was going to enjoy it. Plus, I'd never played an English villain before."

"Miss Croft, it seems
I underestimated you ...
I promise it won't
happen again."

He continues, "I was very taken with the script too. I have had opportunities to make action pictures before but I fought shy of them because I'm not particularly drawn to the genre. It was clear from the first page though that *Tomb Raider* was going to be in a class of its own. All the action was superbly integrated into the story and the characters just flew off the page. The more I read the script, the more I wanted to play Powell because there were so many great character scenes to get my teeth into. Too often the villain in fantasy adventures is just a token baddie but here Powell is intelligent and witty and I relished the fact that he was more than a match for Lara Croft. Powell is a lawyer by trade and that made him very astute in pinpointing people's weaknesses. He spots Lara's Achilles heel immediately and leads her treacherously close to death in a way that's exciting and sexy."

One aspect of *Tomb Raider* Glen had no qualms about at all was the stunt work he had to come to grips with. He says, "I have a pretty flamboyant and lethal sword fight in the film and that was great because I studied fencing at RADA. I was in a class with Ralph (*The English Patient*) Fiennes and we both became obsessed by fencing. All the other students practised for two weeks preparing to show their skills in the graduation Prize Fight in which each was supposed to showcase their acumen at armed and unarmed combat. Ralph

and I practised for two years and our hard work really paid off. I felt really pleased about having so much preparation when I read the sword fight in the script."

Powell, along with Lara's other friends and enemies, were specifically created for the film. None of them exist in the actual game and Glen was pleased about that, as he explains, "I was unfamiliar with the game before we started and I was glad I didn't have to take any baggage from it for my character. No disrespect to the game that hundreds of millions play, but people go and see a film to hear characters speaking, see relationships and situations evolving and to immerse themselves in the exciting story being told. Although Simon West is recreating certain angles from the game, the focus has been to make everything true, real and three-dimensional and expand the concept in very clever ways. Powell goes on a journey that I found very playable because I could trust my own instincts and not be hemmed in by anything that had happened before. As an actor, there was nothing to be gained from immersing myself in the game. I think that's real strength of *Tomb Raider* – it uses the complex language of the game as its basic inspiration but goes way beyond it by incorporating engaging character sub-text, interesting historical fact and startling mysticism all confidently marshalled by Simon West's genius."

## DANIEL CRAIG IS ALEX WEST

Alex West is a mercenary archaeologist who puts himself up for sale to the highest bidder. Initially in *Tomb Raider* his employer is Manfred Powell. But West has a soft spot for Lara Croft, his occasional accomplice, sparring partner and maybe love interest. They meet up again in the bustling lobby of Boothby's Auction House and immediately start arguing over a past expedition in Tibet where Alex "stole" some priceless Prayer Wheels from under her nose. Little does either realize how their fates will inextricably be entwined in the cavernous Tomb of Ten Thousand Shadows.

Daniel Craig plays Alex West and the fast-rising young actor counts *Love Is The Devil*, *Elizabeth*, *I Dreamed Of Africa*, *Some Voices*, *The Trench* and *Hotel Splendide* among his major film credits. The handsome, broad-boned Craig made his film debut straight out of drama school with *The Power Of One*, but it was the BBC television series *Our Friends In The North* that really got him noticed and made his name.

"I like action films as much as anybody else," Craig says. "When the *Tomb Raider* offer came along, I just thought, well, why not? Does it stop me making films that I believe in, or does it raise my profile a little bit so I might have more choice? It was a case of thinking,

are you going to make proper movies or just mess around? Here was a great chance to learn about the blockbuster industry from the best in the business. I would have been mad to turn it down."

There's another reason why Craig wanted to appear in the film too. Unlike the rest of the cast and crew he's a *Tomb Raider* game fanatic. "Sad, but true," he laughs. "I'm an okay player actually and my favourite is *Tomb Raider II*. I was so excited when that was released as I just closed my bedroom curtains and forgot about life for a few weeks. Although *Tomb Raider* bears no real relation to the game, I was thrilled to death when I first walked on to the Pinewood sound stages and looked at the most amazing sets I've ever seen. I'm now a hero to my extended family of game-players. I brought them to the set one day and even now they still can't believe it's real and I'm so close to Lara Croft."

Another key factor in Craig's decision to tackle the part was director Simon West, as he explains. "I love playing comedy and when Simon and I first met to discuss my involvement he told me Alex is pretty funny and doesn't take life too seriously. I thought, well, if I am going to make an action film this is definitely the one to do. I did think Simon's *Con Air* was very humorous for an action film and that was exactly the approach I felt *Tomb Raider* needed and one he was clearly prepared to give it. I've adored playing the massive amounts of irony that comes with Alex's hard man of action surface. Simon told me very specifically what he wanted and I gave it to him. I do love a director who trusts you enough to let you get on with it without droning on too much about character arcs."

Craig also liked the fact that Alex allies himself to both Manfred Powell and Lara Croft at different points in the *Tomb Raider* proceed-ings. He says, "Alex might look like a typical explorer in his combat shorts with a long knife on his belt – he doesn't carry a gun, he borrows Lara's instead – but he's a capitalist at heart. He's in the profession for what he can get and his morals are dubious to say the least. Yet his heart is in the right place and that makes him a fun part to play despite him constantly changing sides. Manfred Powell offers him the opportunity to take the thrill ride of his life, so

work with and very serious about getting it right. Sometimes working with other actors you do get the impression that they're viewing it as just another job. Not Angelina. She has been determined to make something special and has put her own twist on Lara with incredible individuality and style. As a *Tomb Raider* player I can say with absolute authority that she's the perfect Lara Croft."

Because he had never made an action movie before, it was quite hard at first for Craig to get into the rhythm of film making on such an epic scale. He sighs, "You need lots of patience. Filming on The Orrery set (where the giant model of the Solar System was housed) was a nightmare. Because the planets were revolved mechanically, it took ten minutes to re-set each time. So you have to get in the frame of mind where you know you're not going to be doing too much acting, but you have to be ready to spring into action mode when finally called for. While you're mostly sitting around waiting on such days, you still have to maintain your concentration levels and that is absolutely exhausting. Other days I'd go straight into a scene with three pages of dialogue and have to be single-minded about learning it correctly. It's just a different way of working that needs a different mental approach. Once I got into the flow, I realized I could cope with the schedule, but I've never been more tired making a movie."

he jumps at it as most people would. You also get the impression that he wants to go to Cambodia so he can see Lara again. There is a vague history between Alex and Lara as they may, or may not, be ex-lovers. Something has happened in the past that has screwed up their relationship and perhaps Alex wants to try again. It might not happen in this adventure, but as I have signed for two sequels ..."

He adds, "Angelina and I haven't had to work hard to put across the chemistry between us. It has been a breeze. She's smart, intelligent, knows what she's doing and has really stuck her nose to the grindstone. She's ace to

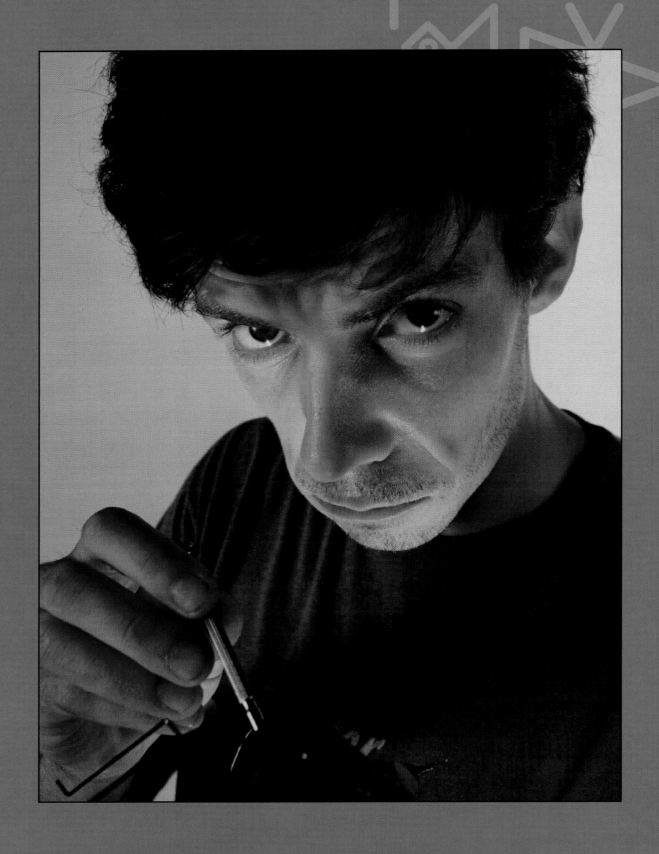

## NOAH TAYLOR IS BRYCE TURING

Bryce Turing is Lara Croft's right-hand man and techno-wizard and the complete antithesis of her physical supremacy. He lives in a messy trailer at Croft Manor surrounded by gadgets, computers and the robotic insect pets he makes out of broken radios and Walkmans as a hobby. Although agony for Bryce is finding himself accompanying Lara on her latest adventure, he knows how much she relies on him for his friendship and technical backup.

Bryce is played by Noah Taylor, best known to worldwide audiences for his role as the young piano prodigy David Helfgott in the award-winning *Shine*. British-born Taylor moved to Australia when very young and won local Best Actor awards for his work in *The Year My Voice Broke*, its sequel *Flirting* and *The Nostradamus Kid*. His other film credits include *Welcome To Woop Woop*, *True Love And Chaos*, *The Road To Alice*, *Prisoner Of St Petersburg* and *Almost Famous*.

"I was at a stage in my career where I wanted to try something different," says Taylor. "I'd never done a blockbuster before and although I knew a little about the *Tomb Raider* games I thought, because Simon West was such an accomplished action director, it would be an interesting education and enjoyable experience. The funny thing about the Bryce charac-

ter was that he was originally Welsh. I think that had a lot to do with Simon being a native Welshman himself. Anyway, I did my audition in a dialect that was more Bangladeshi than Bangor! And, straight after my reading, they changed his accent to being more London non-specific. I didn't know whether to feel insulted or relieved."

Until researching his *Tomb Raider* role, the only cyber prefix Taylor knew anything about was cyber-punk, as he avidly reads the work of William Gibson, author of *Neuromancer* and *All Tomorrow's Parties*. "I'm a committed techno-Luddite really and I can't even change a light bulb," he admits. "I have taken up more of an interest in technology thanks to Bryce, but I'd never become so into it. I think Bryce comes from a hacking background, is something of an anarchist and was probably siphoning off Croft funds from her bank. Rather than report him to the authorities though, she recognized his talents and gave him a job and a home at Croft Manor. My back-story guess is that they've become friends over a ten-year period and have become a crack team through having all these weird adventures together. I wanted to avoid the usual sidekick clichés without going too much against the grain of the territory and I do feel I've successfully etched Bryce as something of a unique damaged unit. Everything Lara wants him to do is a bit of a drag, and he's always moaning, but that dynamic keeps their relationship fresh and interesting. One thing I was determined not to let the wardrobe department do was make me wear a Hawaiian shirt. Have you noticed the computer geek in most films – *Twister* instantly comes to mind – always sports a Hawaiian shirt? What's that all about?"

The one moment in *Tomb Raider* that Taylor feels sums up the relationship between Lara and Bryce comes in the scene where both are trying to unearth the mystery of the clock. He continues, "They know the inside of the clock holds runic clues and directions and Bryce's natural instinct is to take it apart, screw-by-screw, cog-by-cog, and lay it all out in a neat pile. Lara has a more pragmatic approach and she smashes it against the wall. That turns out to be the correct thing to do but in that scene

you immediately grasp the difference between them. Lara instantly makes the right choice other people wouldn't dare consider, while Bryce is precise and meticulous. There's no doubt in my mind though that Bryce loves and respects Lara for that character trait."

By the very nature of his character, Taylor did not have to contend with any major stunt work. He smiles, "I do slide down a ladder and go dog-sledding over a glacier, but that was it apart from some very frightening scenes we filmed on location in Iceland. We had to navigate a lagoon packed with icebergs in these tiny boats and I was scared to death. If you fell in the freezing water, you could have died in two seconds. Although there were people off camera in boats just in case that unlikely event did happen, and everyone kept telling me it was a fairly normal risk for film making purposes, I was absolutely petrified throughout. But then sitting on the swivel chair in Bryce's trailer qualified as a stunt in my estimation!"

Hofn in Iceland was the location for the exteriors of the Tomb of Ten Thousand Shadows. Taylor didn't go to Cambodia as Bryce doesn't figure in that midway section of *Tomb Raider*, but Iceland left a lasting impression on him. He says, "It was an incredible place where you are left in no doubt that nature is the boss. That's the great side to making such an epic film as

## "Angelina fills the screen with her personality. She is the film's best special effect."

you travel to places you'd never normally go to as a tourist. The glacier contained mile-deep crevices that added enormous value to the excitement of the sequence. You couldn't replicate such a landscape using computer-generated imagery and it wouldn't be half so mind-blowing on screen even if you could."

Aside from its computer game inspiration, Taylor feels Simon West has deliberately given *Tomb Raider* a comic book visual look. He explains, "Angelina does a really interesting thing throughout the film. She strikes physical poses that have a classic comic frame stance about them. It gives Lara a larger than life quality which, coupled with her intelligence and beauty, transmits an incredible humanity. It would have been so easy to get someone just to fill the physical requirements of Lara. But if the actress playing her couldn't bring the necessary depth, warmth and human interest to the role, then it would have fallen flat no matter how many fabulous special effects surrounded her. Angelina fills the screen with her personality. She is the film's best special effect."

# JON VOIGHT IS LORD CROFT

Lord Croft (1917–1981) is Lara's late, and sorely missed, father who appears in numerous monochrome flashbacks to guide his strong-willed daughter gently toward the triangle puzzle with parental advice and historically based hints.

Jon Voight plays Lord Croft and is considered to be one of the finest actors of his generation. An Oscar winner for his paraplegic Vietnam veteran in *Coming Home*, he made an early impact, and was nominated for his first Academy Award, in *Midnight Cowboy*. Other early films include *Catch-22*, *Deliverance*, *Conrack* and *The Odessa File*. More recently he has appeared in *Mission: Impossible*, *Anaconda*, *Enemy of the State* and *Pearl Harbor*. His third Oscar nomination was for *Runaway Train* and he is the very proud father of *Tomb Raider* star Angelina Jolie.

"Angie and I have talked about working together before," says Voight, "but neither of us saw the *Tomb Raider* opportunity that was right under our noses until the last minute. Originally, when we discussed this film, it seemed the best approach was not to bring it so close to home. I didn't want to rain on her parade as she was the star so I made alternative casting suggestions. Then, after obviously talking it over with Simon West, she rang me about the possibility saying 'It's a good call, so don't worry' and, naturally, I was delighted. But I wanted her to be absolutely sure she had the right person and would be comfortable playing opposite her own father. The last thing I wanted to happen was our professional relationship interfering with our tight family one."

He continues, "I have always known Angie had a strong personality and that we were a bit alike in the way we approach things. So I thought two hard-headed people like us might end up banging against each other and I was nervous. It turned out to be exactly the opposite as we worked perfectly together, developing our characters, their shared emotions and humour. Simon helped us towards that goal and, frankly, I was surprised by his even temper and brightness, because of his big, heavy-action past. But he helped us both get the right balance necessary with patience and warmth. He doesn't allow things to get to him and that's precisely the sort of director you need to pull off such a vast undertaking as *Tomb Raider*."

Voight is particularly fond of his and Angelina's first scenes together, as he remarks. "We had this eye-to-eye talking sequence that was both intimate and magical because it's where Croft's past meets Lara's present. We worked on it prior to shooting and I was amazed at her clarity and how insightful and exciting her thoughts were. She dazzled me with her professional understanding and her willingness to explore our own private relationship to add authenticity to the characters' bond. It's something to savour when you can tell your own daughter how you feel about her on film. Obviously, I'm so proud when I watch Angie on screen, but watching her perform up close is something else. You can vividly see the emotional risks she's taking and her charismatic determination."

When Angelina first described the character of Lord Croft to her father, she told him she viewed the part as "a bit like Barry and your dad". Voight explains, "Barry is my volcanologist brother who is one of the world's leading authorities on lava flow. He puts himself at great risk to save people and villages affected by eruptions. I've always seen him as a hero and Angie saw Croft as the same kind of inquisitive adventurer. My father was a wonderful storyteller and Angie has kept tapes of him relating all these great tales revolving around

humour and ethics. They weren't supposed to be educational but she has learnt a lot from them. So the scenes we have together echo my father too. But I was touched the most when Croft had a line in the movie saying, 'You can't be caged or made to sit and listen to old dusty rules, you come alive in pursuit and you can't change who you are'. Angie took me aside and whispered, 'Forget what I said about Barry and your father, Croft is just you, dad'. I was very moved by that comment."

Voight was cast quite late in the proceedings, but if he had any fears about being the newcomer among an already tight and focused crew, they were dispelled the moment he arrived at the happy environment at Pinewood Studios. He adds, "It's often a strange experience to suddenly appear in the middle of a well-oiled and relaxed operation. I got straight off the plane and the first person I met was costume designer Lindy Hemming, who gave me the warmest welcome, a big hug and started telling jokes. It was just what I needed to get me into the swing of things. I have worked at Pinewood before, on *Mission: Impossible*, and I can't tell you how much I adore the people who work in the British Film Industry. The standard of professionalism and craftsmanship in Britain really is second to none."

Being Angelina's father first and foremost meant that Voight was ever watchful of his daughter's safety during her stunt scenes. He

There she was on top of this broken column, surrounded by Egyptian art, fighting this monster and she pulled out these guns and started flipping them around with both hands. I had never seen anybody do anything like it and I loved the fact it was my daughter setting a new action standard."

## CHRIS BARRIE IS HILLARY

Hillary is Lara Croft's very proper English butler who tries his level-headed best to protect his mistress and is just as handy firing a pump-action shotgun as he is tending his beloved bonsai plants.

admits, "I was always telling her to protect herself properly, be careful and ensure all the stunt risks were kept to a minimum. I like doing the physical stuff too and have injured myself in the past. But she's approached the arduous aspects in the same professional fashion she has everything else and I can really tell she's having fun exploring that side of filming an epic fantasy adventure. The first time I saw her in Lara Croft's costume was incredible.

Chris Barrie plays Hillary and he enjoys cult status in British television for the long-running series *Red Dwarf* and *The Brittas Empire*. He began his television career as one of the voices in the satirical puppet show *Spitting Image*, imitating such world figures as Prince Charles and Ronald Reagan, and is a veteran of the British alternative comedy scene. *Tomb Raider* is Barrie's first film.

"When I first met Simon West about the Hillary role, he told me he was looking for one part of a double-act," recalls Barrie. "He wanted someone who could form a sort of Laurel and Hardy relationship with the Bryce character. I had no idea why he thought of me, except thinking Hugh (*101 Dalmatians*, *Jeeves and Wooster*) Laurie probably wasn't available! All I knew at that point was both characters were Lara's sidekicks at Croft Manor. As it wasn't the first time I'd been cast in the slightly stiffer, more disciplined role, one playing off a wilder, messier and more laid-back counterpart, I knew I could do the job well. I didn't hear anything for weeks and I was just about to accept a BBC film when suddenly my agent called and said I had to sign the *Tomb Raider* contract by that night if I still wanted it. It was so dramatic! As the BBC offer was virtually a watered down version of my *Brittas* character, there was no contest and I became part of this huge mega-movie. I'd heard of the game mainly through some friends' children who were almost surgically linked to their computer consoles through playing it non-stop, but I knew nothing about it except the name of Lara Croft. When I started on the film, I got this fantastic 'Welcome Aboard' pack from Paramount which was a rucksack containing a survival kit, food rations and a few *Tomb Raider* games. Now I have no excuse not to play it!"

"I think Hillary is quite a cool customer," continues Barrie. "He knew Lord Croft and sees his prime directive as protecting Lara. He is a slightly anally retentive, petty-minded fusspot who tries to keep Croft manor in good order despite Bryce continually trashing the place. He practices Tai Chi and grows bonsai plants to keep grounded in this house of relative madness. The joy of playing Hillary is that all this builds up to his defining moment when he gets out the shotgun and blasts his way down the corridor. Secretly I think that's what he's been eagerly waiting to happen all along. Moments like that remove the character from being a typical movie butler, like Alfred in *Batman*, for example. I don't like calling Hillary a butler anyway – he's more a personal assistant figure in my mind. Because I had no time to prepare for the part, I was so grateful when Angelina got Noah Taylor and myself together in the first week of shooting and said, 'Right, let's get this family sorted out here'. After that we looked like we had known each other for years."

Because *Tomb Raider* was Barrie's feature film debut, he was rather relieved to find a very relaxed atmosphere on the set. He says, "You hear so many horror stories about making films as vast as this but Simon's calmness has filtered down to everyone. He has a very easy going approach that I now realize is essential to create a conducive atmosphere for good work on such an epic adventure. There's nothing worse, when you are trying to do some-

**OPPOSITE**: Lara and her "family": Hillary and Bryce.

thing tricky, to suddenly find the director breathing down your neck saying, 'We didn't do it this way earlier in the week now did we, luvvie?' None of that irksomeness has happened here."

Angelina Jolie's professionalism also helped Barrie control the butterflies in his stomach too. He explains, "She's prepared for just about anything that anyone wants to throw at her. Lara is an extraordinarily challenging role aside from learning the stunts, the bungee ballet and enunciating an English accent. I found her dedication awesome and inspiring. Plus, she's a nice, normal decent girl with it. I've enjoyed every minute of working with her. Lara Croft is really James Bond and Indiana Jones rolled into one and for my money she's definitely more attractive in the form of Angelina than she is in the original game."

## JULIAN RHIND-TUTT IS MR PIMMS

As Manfred Powell's law clerk, Mr Pimms affects a studied, solicitous manner leavened with a unique gawky humour as he grudgingly

accompanies his boss to the far-flung corners of the globe. Julian Rhind-Tutt plays Mr Pimms and he enjoyed an early springboard success in the hit play *The Madness of George III* and later in the screen version, *The Madness of King George*. He also appeared in *The Saint, Tomorrow Never Dies, Les Miserables, Notting Hill, Sword of Honour* and *The Trench*, the latter two films also featuring fellow *Tomb Raider* actor Daniel Craig.

"Mr Pimms is on the cusp of good," says Rhind-Tutt about his character. "Manfred Powell is a lawyer when he's not being an arch villain and I'm his dogsbody assistant in court when not helping him to be a nasty baddie. I'm there to give light relief to the serious moments. I think he's basically a good guy who's stumbled into the job because of a work experience assignment. I became Powell's pupil, studying to be a barrister, when suddenly I'm dragged into his nefarious schemes and have to watch people die horrible deaths. Naturally, Mr Pimms is taken aback by that, but too scared to walk away and inflame Powell's wrath. I'm the hapless observer who constantly stands back in amazement rather than wield a knife. It's been easy to work with Iain Glen and build up a rapport because I've known him for

RIGHT: Rogues gallery: Manfred Powell, Alex West and Mr Pimms in Cambodia.

a while. Iain's brother-in-law is a good friend and I've lodged with him and his wife."

When Rhind-Tutt first met Simon West, he knew he was up for one of either two parts in *Tomb Raider*. He continues, "They hadn't cast Hillary or Mr Pimms and I had no idea which part he had in mind for me. Two months later we met again, had a brief conversation about my going to Warwick University – he had once shared a flat with Warwick students – and he offered me Mr Pimms. Simon told me he didn't want the usual comedic incompetent that was the cinematic tradition for the stock villainous subordinate. He wanted a character with a real identity to give a more convincing basis for the action. I feel I fulfilled that brief along with the rest of the excellent *Tomb Raider* cast, who also refused to conform to action figure ciphers."

The one regret Rhind-Tutt has about *Tomb Raider* is that he only has a couple of scenes with Angelina Jolie. He explains, "I don't have a lot to do with Lara Croft because she's in her group and I'm in Powell's. But Angelina has impressed me with her discipline, thoughts and ideas for the greater good of the whole movie. There's been an easy camaraderie among the actors because we're all facing the unknown together as none of us have ever been involved in something so huge based on an even more enormous slice of pop culture history."

He adds, "What was funny was that I kept being recognized more than Angelina when we went to Iceland. I happened to be on television twice during our stay there – in a TV series I'd done years before titled *Hippies*. I couldn't walk down the streets without being stopped for my autograph. So, at least, I'm bigger than Angelina in Iceland!"

The most important thing Simon West conveyed to Rhind-Tutt was that he saw Mr Pimms as the eye of the audience. He adds, "That's because I have no fighting or hands-on combat. I just run away and look aghast. Simon is the best all round director I've come across because he has a visual brilliance for the action genre, thoroughly enjoys his job and makes sure everyone else enjoys theirs too. *Tomb Raider* is the biggest film I'm ever likely to be involved with and it's great to get the experience of making a massive Hollywood epic without having to go there to do it. You don't often get the chance to see Chinook helicopters flying ten feet above your head thirty-seven times in a row. It's all the skilled technicians who have amazed me with their expertise and professionalism on this show. And these are the people you never see get the proper credit. Just watching the special effects experts map out the Tomb of the Dancing Light to the last pixel on a computer screen is awe-inspiring. If I'm stunned by it – and I'm in the movie – I can't imagine how thrilled audiences are going to be when they see it for the first time."

**OPPOSITE**: The Tomb of the Dancing Light: Lara drops in unexpectedly.

# 5

# THE LOOK

## THE COSTUMES

**ABOVE:** Three very different looks for Lara: ready for action in Iceland, contemplative in Cambodia and fearless, forty feet above the floor.

Costume designer Lindy Hemming was completely up to speed on the whole Lara Croft phenomenon before she even started working on *Tomb Raider*. It was Hemming who dressed Denise Richards as a Lara Croft clone in *The World Is Not Enough* for her role as Dr Christmas Jones. "I'm sure that's why all the rumours started circulating about Denise being in the casting running for *Tomb Raider*," says Hemming. "I knew about Lara Croft because I have three teenage children and I thought it was an obvi-

ous contemporary look for Denise, one that streetwise audiences would instantly recognize."

Hemming worked on the previous two Bond movies, *GoldenEye* and *Tomorrow Never Dies*, and had just won an Oscar for her costume design in Mike Leigh's *Topsy Turvy* when she received the *Tomb Raider* offer. She says, "I had met Simon West a few weeks before the Oscar ceremony and we struck up an instant rapport because we both come from Wales. I told him to go for someone younger, but I think the

Oscar clinched it. Two days after winning the Academy Award I was officially asked to join the production."

If Hemming thought her *Topsy Turvy* workload was an enormous undertaking – sixty principal characters in authentic Victorian garb – her *Tomb Raider* assignment was even harder. She explains, "Most of my budget went on duplication, overnight mending and fabrication. For example, one T-shirt that became the Lara Croft staple (a Red Hot Chili Pepper label design customized on the neck and shoulder lines) had to have sixty copies in grey, white and black to cope with on-set wear and tear and also provide the stuntwomen with exact fire-resistant replicas. While we weren't required to produce the costume look as per the game, we couldn't swerve too far away from Lara's traditional cut-down shorts, tank top and boots."

Ten weeks prior to principal photography, Hemming met Angelina Jolie once a week to discuss Lara's look and what the actress would feel comfortable wearing. She says, "I had an image of what Lara should look like but Angelina needed to find her character in the midst of that. She was very strong-minded about what she wasn't going to wear and equally clear on the way she wanted Lara presented. As Angelina's own artistic perception of Lara arrived quite late in pre-production a lot of costume decisions couldn't be made because she wasn't ready to make them. It did make my

job difficult but I'm in no way critical of Angelina's working methods. I mean she will probably have to have the same image in two further films so she was determined to get it right the first time. Angelina is not the sort of person who wears torn jeans or tomboy clothes in real life. She's a precise, minimal person who loves wearing simple chic clothes and her own taste had to be echoed in Lara's tight-stretch trousers and sleeveless silhouette or she wasn't going to feel at ease acting. Angelina is a proper actress – not a starlet – and I was impressed by how much thought and emotional investment she put into Lara's wardrobe."

She continues, "Angelina is a very body-conscious, physically strong girl and her own fashion colour schemes are always monochromatic. She is very colour aware and knows what suits her. She will never wear green, for example. I'd have been crazy not to take on board what she knew she looked best in. It actually worked out extremely well in the long run because all the other characters are in colours and her darker-spectrum look not only accented her luminous eyes but also gave Lara a separateness, an otherworldly feel that was perfect for the film."

Hemming explains the finer points of Lara's wardrobe: "Lara's trousers were made by Melanie Apple, a small ladies sportswear manufacturer in Los Angeles. Thankfully, the company were prepared to alter, remake, change the length, add padding to disguise stunt har-

Motorcycle 1960s look, and made by a bondage-wear tailor. Her dog-sled outfit is a luxurious suede coat with an asymmetrical fur collar to match the huskies' colouring. That's very *Dr Zhivago*. Her bungee ballet pyjamas are martial arts influenced. But my favourite costume of all has to be the one she wears in Cambodia. After talking to monks and taking a shower, she puts on her stylish version of their orange silk robes. It's like she's wearing a designer sari and I think it captures Angelina at her most beautiful."

For the rest of the cast's outfits Hemming found herself shopping in the world's trendiest stores. She says, "Manfred Powell has the most expensive wardrobe because he's an elegant wealthy lawyer. We kitted Iain Glen out in a $7,000 Prada curly lamb grey coat, shoes and knitwear, Issey Miyake sportswear, Yohji Yamamoto and Kenzo suits and Gucci sweaters. We had to copy Iain's shiny black Miyake ski tracksuit he wears in The Orrery thirty times over to cope with all the bullet hits planned for the garment.

I saw the Mr Pimms character as not so much an old fogey as a new one so I mixed basic City-type Paul Smith shirts with Vivienne Westwood and Katharine Hamnett designs for Julian Rhind-Tutt. He was actually a fan of Westwood clothes so it was a great look for him. I do like his beige safari suit with red stripes – very tongue-in-chic!"

Daniel Craig, Noah Taylor and Jon Voight were the easiest to dress says Hemming. "Alex is the

nesses and then ship the finished product overnight to London in all different weights – thickest for Iceland and thinnest for Cambodia. Along with the T-shirt, these trousers are part of a survival kit Lara takes on journeys in her rucksack. She's like Superman – she can dress for action in an instant. Her rucksack and belt-buckle are Futori Design. Lara's shoes were designed by me with big soles and made by 1970s Chelsea fashion king Terry De Havilland. Her motorbike outfit was a two-piece suit, based on pop star Marianne Faithfull's *Girl On A* modern day rugged action hero who the audience is not supposed to like at first but gradually warms to. So his initial auction house outfit is Giorgio Armani and his Cambodian look is Gap shorts or bootleg cut Levi 507s, very expensive RN Williams boots and sexy Calvin Klein white vests to show off his body. Bryce is a grunge fashion nightmare so Noah wears all second-hand jeans and T-shirts. For Lord Croft I

designer Kirk Petruccelli heard the duo were about to embark on *Tomb Raider*. "I knew the game," says Petruccelli, "and I thought it would be such an exciting challenge that I begged them to put my name forward to Simon West. They were convinced he would choose a British designer because it was a Pinewood Studios-based production. He couldn't find the right person though, so we met up,

looked at pictures of explorer Sir Ranulph Fiennes as reference material, then combed Los Angeles thrift stores for an old leather jacket, polo neck shirt and American chinos. I feel each of the characters has their own separate iconic look to compliment Lara's unique appearance."

## THE SET DESIGN

It was while working on the comic book spoof *Mystery Men*, also produced by Lawrence Gordon and Lloyd Levin, that production

hit it off and I was suddenly involved in the biggest assignment, both in scope and scale, of my entire career."

Coming from a background of fine arts and graphic design, Petruccelli worked as assistant art director on numerous pictures before taking his first production designer credit, on *Three Ninjas*, in 1992. His films since then include *Anaconda*, *Blade*, *The Thirteenth Floor* and *The Patriot*. Petruccelli describes his *Tomb Raider* look as "Super-contemporary – a mix of pre-antiquity and classic Tudor architecture –

**ABOVE**: Building the sets for *Tomb Raider*.

smashed through with attainable modern. Simon didn't want anything stereotypical and, although the design is quite stylized, he was adamant nothing should look too futuristic. Simon had a keen visual grasp of what was needed, and the atmosphere he wanted cinematographer Peter Menzies to capture, and gave me some key phrases and metaphors to build on, the main one being 'the advanced fantastic rooted in modern reality'. Of course, I always had to bear in mind the game, but there were no real design guidelines in that department. The only aspects I discussed with Eidos and Core Design were Lara's Norton motorbike and her Land Rover. Once they approved those illustrations, they were happy."

There were three enormous set designs Petruccelli calls "equal parts stimulating and daunting" on *Tomb Raider*. He continues, "The

main hall at Croft Manor was an interesting conception. One half had to be typical Elizabethan in the grand historical manner, with an imposing staircase and gallery, the other half – divided by a floor-to-ceiling glass wall – had to house Lara's brightly-lit base of computer operations, complete with high-tech control panels and sleek monitors. The fittings in the first half were constructed out of rubber, so Angelina and the stuntmen wouldn't hurt themselves if they accidentally crashed into anything during the bungee ballet. The lighting was the most important part of the Space Age half so Lara could control night and day within that environment."

Petruccelli's two other major set constructions were built inside Pinewood's famous 007 sound stage. Both The Orrery, housed within the Tomb of Ten Thousand Shadows, and the vast temple interior of the Tomb of the Dancing Light occupied Europe's largest soundstage. He continues, "The Orrery was devised as a minimalist grotto using a mainly black, blue and white colour scheme inspired by Iceland's glacier-rich landscape. Within that we had to construct the giant, fully operational, metallic Solar System on which the main protagonists battle and climb around. It had a 180-foot wingspan and had to travel in four different directions at between three and fifteen miles an hour. I based it on strong circular geometry surrounded by super-ancient materials as the entire subterranean set was supposed to have

been created five thousand years ago by a crashed meteor. I asked some real scientists to explain how the Earth would have taken such an impact and included that texture advice to make the set look timeless."

However, Petruccelli's crowning achievement is the Tomb of the Dancing Light, where Lara swings from the roof on a log and pierces an altar urn, causing a column of liquid mercury to flood everywhere. Originally, this action sequence was planned to take place on the Great Wall of China. He explains, "We were going to build a section of the wall in Scotland and augment it with digital special effects. But Simon not only wanted a more lush, styled environment for this major action highlight but also somewhere that hadn't been seen before. So when one of my supervising art directors, Les Tomkins, suggested Cambodia we looked into how tolerant the authorities would be for a film crew to go there. The hurdles didn't look that insurmountable and it proved to be the perfect contrast to cold Iceland."

He continues, "The Tomb of the Dancing Light took sixteen weeks to build based on two hundred and fifty illustrations, with thirty set designers overseeing the construction and three hundred plasterers, painters, carpenters and riggers working around the clock. In terms of size, detail and the time frame, it is the biggest set I've ever had to design. My art directors (Les Tomkins, John Fenner, Jim Morahan and David Lee) and I went on a recce to Cambodia to view the temple at Angkor Wat so we could include the architectural motifs and grey sandstone colouring in the set. No overt colour was used so as not to detract from Lara's spectacular arrival. We made the Tomb a cruciform shape in the classic church design, then dug into it to allow for the different planes, lengths and levels Simon needed for his action backdrop."

always make it look visually interesting and different to any film seen before."

## THE SPECIAL EFFECTS

"I actively sought out *Tomb Raider*," says special effects supervisor Chris Corbould. "The moment I heard it was being made, I rushed out and bought *Tomb Raider: The Last Revelation* and became totally obsessed by it for four months. Just by playing the game I could see the potential for creating some of the wildest special effects ever and I was at a point in my career where I wanted to do something less realistic than James Bond and well away from the desert sands of *The Mummy*. I'm a real fan of fantasy adventure and, because the main lead was female, I thought *Tomb Raider* had the potential to cast the genre in a totally new light."

He adds, "The idea was to give it a strong architectural grid and then destroy that organic movement with almost floating circles, like the central dais, balconies and giant Buddha altar. The set was made out of scaffolding and plaster with real stone on the floors, polystyrene route systems allowing movement throughout, and plaster texturing. The ceilings were vacu-formed to make them as light as possible and the monkey statues – inspired by the actual Khmer monkey god – lining the walls were made out of fibreglass to ensure their mobility. None of the hieroglyphics or prayer iconography is based on anything we saw in Cambodia for fear of insulting their sacred religions. You must always be cognizant of that side of things when you invade another culture. The whole set was flexible and interchangeable with built-in lighting so Simon could stage the action in a number of areas to

Since the early 1990s Corbould has become a major name in the special effects arena by working on some of the most demanding big budget productions. Inspired to enter the field by his uncle, Colin Chilvers (an effects veteran responsible for *Superman* and *The Rocky Horror Picture Show*), Corbould added his own trademark magic to *GoldenEye*, *Tomorrow Never Dies*, *The World Is Not Enough* and *102 Dalmatians*. Working in close collaboration with digital effects supervisor Steve Begg and stunt coordinator Simon Crane, it's Corbould who achieved all the weirdness Simon West needed for his spectacular scenario. He adds, "Simon West wanted fantastic camera angles to shoot from and truly bizarre visuals. He's very much a spur of the moment director and often widened my brief after seeing the great results we were getting. For example, Lara swinging on the log in the Tomb of the Dancing Light triggered more ideas for further action shots and it was up to me to devise them, often overnight."

In the order they appear in *Tomb Raider*, these are the main effects Corbould devised throughout twenty weeks of preparation and another twenty-four in production. "The first major scene is the droid fight between Lara and a ten-foot metal *Terminator*-like robot. This was a blend of computer graphics with a fair amount of close-up business to show the droid punching through sarcophaguses, destroying valuable antiques and receiving bullet hits. It was done in quick shots using basic puppeteering, although we did build a proper robot from scratch with all the mechanics so Lara could drag it down steps to show Bryce.

"Bryce's trailer has all these robotic insects scuttling around as Simon West wanted to instantly convey his nerdy, but inventive, character. He showed me videos of these mechanical creatures people had made as hobbies and asked me for ideas. We came up with six different robotic flies, spiders and caterpillars made out of odd bits of electrical equipment and Simon liked them so much he requested four more. One thing we had to be careful about was the use of mobile phones on the set. They can often trigger pre-planned explosions. So if anyone was caught using one on any of the soundstages, they were dumped in a bucket of water by the door.

"The bungee ballet provided us with a rather interesting challenge. Simon West wanted to keep Angelina's face in full frame as she runs around the walls, bounces from the ceiling and

**LEFT AND OVERLEAF:** One of the most impressive sequences sees Lara battle Bryce's droid.

ties up the intruders searching for the vital clock. Rather than just have the camera pan around from a central position, we built a camera rig on a thirty-four-foot diameter arm attached to a hydraulic turntable that could track around any part of the room with her at four revolutions a minute. It was an essentially simple solution to the problem but it looks stunning as you vividly witness every moment of Lara's physical exhilaration. Angelina is the gutsiest actress I've ever worked with and she has made our work look fabulous.

"The chain reaction in the Tomb of the Dancing Light involved a hugely complex interaction between my crew, Simon Crane and the CGI guys. Lara climbs on to a log suspended from the ceiling, it swings down across the whole length of the Tomb with gun shots ringing around her, eventually pierces the urn in the giant Buddha's lap, which releases a cascade of water uncovering a bank of phosphorous. That explodes, the heat created expands a mercury column that rises up from the central dais, pours down the walls, falls on the monkey warrior statues lining the walls and sparks them to life. While the mercury reaction and the monkey soldiers are all digitally created, we had to destroy large parts of the set to make it look as realistic as possible. Definitely the most complicated sequence. Because we moved in real time and shot in continuity to avoid any nightmare logistics, this took us two months to shoot.

"The sequence containing the most effects work was The Orrery. The metallic Solar System had to revolve on four different axes, containing three planets each, at varying speeds – three miles per hour on the inside, fifteen on the outside. The whole construction weighed twenty-eight tons, was powered by four hydraulic motors linked back to a computer system and power pack as big as a small truck to ensure the movement was exactly the same each time. The hardest thing was getting the spinning planets not to crash into each other as there was only a six-inch gap between them. This was the very first sequence we started planning right from the beginning because we knew how complicated it was going to be.

"After getting the triangle piece from the centre of the Sun, Lara and Alex must get out of the Tomb by avoiding falling stalagmites. Simon West wanted to increase the tension by using visuals similar to *The Matrix* – having the sharp rock shapes drop in slow motion at varying speeds from the point of view of the characters as they run around them. This was achieved by building a circular track for a three thousand frames-per-second photo-sonic camera travelling at twenty-two miles per hour past a fifteen-foot falling stalagmite. It's a terrific effect that I feel outdoes *The Matrix* in purely visceral terms.

"Added to that, when The Orrery finally collapses, a huge tidal wave floods through the main archway and engulfs the Tomb, which Lara and Alex escape from by causing time to stand still and running underneath the crest. To achieve the perfect wave we dumped seventy tons of water down a forty-foot ramp and filmed it in slow motion. It took us ages adjusting the ramp and ironing out any obstructions so the curve at the bottom would be enough for the characters to realistically duck under. In some tests the wave went up too sharply, in others it flattened off too quickly. It took us three weeks to get the right angle and precise wave form but it was worth all the effort as such embellishments make *Tomb Raider* sizzle.

## THE STUNTS

Working on *Tomb Raider* came as something of a relief to stunt coordinator Simon Crane. He explains, "When you work on pictures like *Saving Private Ryan*, *Titanic* and *Vertical Limit*, you are reined in by realism and fact. The hardest stunt I've ever had to pull off was in *Saving Private Ryan*, showing someone getting shot while running and falling flat on their face. *Tomb Raider* meant I could go to town as it was pure adrenaline-pumping Hollywood-style action all the way."

After a career as a stunt double for such actors as Timothy Dalton (*The Living Daylights*), Mel Gibson (*Air America*) and Kevin Costner (*Robin Hood: Prince Of Thieves*), Crane performed stunts in many movies, including *Indiana Jones And The Last Crusade*, *Alien 3* and *Total Recall*. He then became a stunt arranger for movies such as *Cliffhanger*, *Braveheart* and *The World Is Not Enough*. Not content with one *Tomb Raider* job, Crane also took the role of second unit director.

"Obviously my job is a lot easier when stars do their own stunts," says Crane. "But you can never allow them to take safety risks even though they will always want to push their limits. I had to be quite strict with Angelina because if she sustained even the slightest injury it would halt production ... She was brilliant in the bungee ballet and triple somersaulted forty feet up in the air. She really sells everything she does

and if her acting career should ever dry up she definitely could have a future in stunt work."

Three months prior to shooting, Crane tested out all his ideas on video and showed Simon West the results. He continues, "That way we could fine tune anything on Simon's request while ensuring everything planned is both physically possible and totally safe. It's a constant headache trying to go one better on each successive film. Here we've done that with Lara's motorbike sequence where she makes a sixty-foot long jump at a height of eighteen feet over a million pound's worth of top range cars in the confined area of her equipment room. As she jumps, her heads scrapes the roof and some cars blow up. We had to make sure Kirk Petruccelli designed the set with removable walls so we could get up to the right speed."

Crane did get a games expert to lead him around the *Tomb Raider* universe to show what he was up against from the fighting point of view. He says, "We are using certain moves from the games – taken ten steps further – but I didn't want to simply rehash the computer action as Simon was clear on everything being totally original. Lara's fighting style in the film is street fighter mixed with martial arts. She hits her victims only once – not bang, bang, bang – for more realism and to make her seem invincible. She hits hard and fast with a purpose for maximum realism without resorting to comedy moves. The biggest challenge for me concerned

the fact that Angelina is left-handed. So all the stunts had to be designed to take that into account and all the stunt men and women had to be trained in left-handed manoeuvres. That was tricky."

So was actually getting on the vast sets to practice, recalls Crane. "The stunts planned for the Tomb of the Dancing Light were quite complex and I asked for six days rehearsal with the actors. Because the set took longer being built than anyone had expected, all I got was six hours. That's where Angelina's rigid training programme really paid dividends as she didn't need too much intensive rehearsal. In some ways I wish her costumes had sported more long sleeves to minimize any bruising – the makeup department wouldn't have spent so much time covering up her tattoos – but Angelina was a real trouper and one of the most proficient athletes I've ever had the pleasure of working with."

**BELOW**: Manfred Powell and Alex West tackle a bit of tomb raiding.

# PART SIX:

# TOMB RAIDER ON LOCATION

"It was a voyage
of total discovery..."

IAIN GLEN

**" I not only wanted audiences to see something new in the *Tomb Raider* story, I also wanted to take them to places they have never seen before ..."**

SIMON WEST

Lara Croft took her first steps on to celluloid on July 31, 2000. On that day director Simon West called "Action!" for the very first time on *Tomb Raider* based at London's Pinewood Studios. In the course of the next arduous six months of principal photography, West's handpicked cast and crew travelled to extremes of environment and climate to ensure Lara's inaugural screen adventure hit every possible high note of turbo-charged action and epic fantasy. From the stunningly alien landscape of Hofn in Iceland, where Lara takes control of a team of wild huskies for an exhilarating race across a vast glacier, to the sultry forests of Cambodia and the twelfth-century temples at Angkor Wat, *Tomb Raider* offered West the broadest canvas on which to paint his stunning event movie.

The Painted Hall at Greenwich's Royal Naval College in London stood in for Venice, where *Tomb Raider* begins. Simon West says, "I like films to open with an attention-grabbing splash and our first scene introduces the *Illuminati* secret society, plus bad guy Manfred Powell, and strongly hints at the other-worldly drama, pyrotechnics and excitement to come. We could have gone to Venice but rather than spend money doing that, I chose to film closer to home and fill the scene with extras for the best screen value."

Other locations used to give *Tomb Raider* its heightened reality look included London's Battersea Power Station (where Powell exacts sadistic vengeance in his own inimitable fashion), Salisbury Plain – the home of the druid Stonehenge – where Royal Air Force Chinook helicopters crowded the skies, and Dulwich College's main assembly hall, which became the interior of Boothby's Auction House (for added authenticity, a real Sotheby's auctioneer agreed to take the bids).

The famous marble folly Elvedon Hall doubled as Powell's townhouse. "I loved my country pad location," says Iain Glen. "It's now owned by the Guinness family although it was

**OPPOSITE AND ABOVE:** London's Battersea Power Station provided a dramatic backdrop for a sinister scene involving Powell, Pimms and Wilson.
**OPPOSITE, INSET:** Dulwich College was transformed into Boothby's Auction House in an early scene.

**ABOVE AND OPPOSITE:** *Tomb Raider* took cast and crew to some remarkable locations including Iceland which stood in for Siberia.

designed by an eccentric maharaja from the Punjab and is just astonishing. It was used in the Second World War as an upmarket billet for American air force officers and its glorious flamboyancy was perfect to put across the type of person Powell is. All these mysterious background characters are seen doing some very dodgy things and such an oddly designed location made that seem almost normal."

Lara's ancestral home Croft Manor was a combination of exteriors filmed at Hatfield House in Hertfordshire and a lavish baronial interior and computer room built in Pinewood's 007 sound stage. "We were going to burn down Croft Manor at one point in the game series," confides Core Design's Adrian Smith, "but we eventually decided not to because we had a strong feeling the filmmakers would

want to use the location. I'm glad we made that decision as the games fans are going to be thrilled to see it in such wonderful detail."

Not just game fans either, as the Croft Manor set completely knocked out co-star Noah Taylor when he walked on to it for the first time. "The problem with sets generally is they feel like sets and what's meant to be stone is made from polystyrene and looks it. But the Croft Manor interior just blew me away as the idea of one half being old world architecture and the other half being super hi-tech works brilliantly well. It has been easy to believe that Lara, Bryce and Hillary live there and that has added enormously to our character relationships. Production designer Kirk Petruccelli has done a marvellous job and every visitor has commented on the *Tomb Raider* sets being the best they've seen in ages. The Tomb of the Dancing Light is also incredibly spectacular and goes beyond anything I've seen on film. The sets are classic British constructions in the James Bond tradition and reminded me of both *Dr No* and *You Only Live Twice*."

Chris Barrie agrees with Taylor. "The sheer expertise on show is what never ceases to amaze me. I've had to pinch myself so many times before filming scenes with Angelina and Noah because I couldn't believe they had just built these extraordinary sets for our movie. You walk into this vast back lot shed and there's a house you immediately feel at home in, which creates a marvellous atmosphere for us to work with." Jon Voight was equally struck by the sets and, when he wasn't filming his scenes, even went so far as to spend time with the crew artists who painted them. He continues, "I really think they should put some of the crew's work in an art exhibition and not tell anyone where they came from. I'm certain they would be treated with the same artistic respect as the work of our famous masters. There are some backdrops I'd love to put on the walls of my own house! The effort taken by these artisans so that Simon West can walk on the set, absorb the beauty and atmosphere, and be inventive with his

camera movements, has impressed me enormously. I took full advantage of my time off and wandered around each department like I was visiting a theme park! I was amused, fascinated and learnt a lot."

However, if the set constructions at Pinewood stunned the cast, the global exteriors racked up a few more notches on the amazement scale.

"I not only wanted audiences to see something new in the *Tomb Raider* story, I also wanted to take them to places they have never seen before. I want *Tomb Raider* to have a constant 'Wow' factor and the locations certainly provide that. Modern audiences are so used to seeing such exotic locations as Egypt or the Far East these days and I wanted to be more adventurous and really surprise them. I chose Iceland to double as Siberia for our climax and Cambodia to provide us with other rarely seen environments," says director, Simon West

"Hofn in Iceland was tough to work in," recalls Iain Glen, "as we were filming on top of this huge glacier the size of Wales. You really felt you were at the ends of the Earth because it was so alien looking and desolate. We spent three days manoeuvring vehicles down a mountainside on to the glacier that would suddenly have icebergs dramatically breaking

away from it and floating gently toward the edge. I would never have gone to Iceland if it hadn't been for *Tomb Raider* and that is one of the gifts of film making because it takes you to these far-flung, fabulous places that you would never normally go."

Daniel Craig has a specific reminiscence of Iceland too. "Originally we were going to charge across the glacier in four-wheel drive Land Rovers. But when we got to Iceland, Simon West suddenly saw these amphibious landing craft vehicles, called 'ducks', and wanted to use those instead as they could traverse any terrain on both water and land. I had a scene where one of the 'ducks' starts to move and I jump on to it from a couple of feet away. Well, I missed, and got dragged along the ice until I awkwardly hoisted myself up. It wasn't easy trying to act cool after that. I was surprised how dangerous Iceland actually was. There were huge crevasses everywhere and we always had to have a safety officer with us to guide our pathway through the ice. We had to take more precautions than usual, which slowed us down a bit."

If Iceland was an exciting adventure for the cast and crew, Cambodia surpassed it in every respect. "It was a voyage of total discovery," remarks Iain Glen. "It touched us all in a profound way. The country also provides a spiritual heart to *Tomb Raider* that goes way beyond any of our performances." Unseen on film for thirty-six years (Cambodian-set movies like *The Killing Fields* were shot in neighbouring Thailand) because of the Vietnam War in the 1960s, Pol Pot and his Khmer Rouge dictatorship in the 1970s and a civil war in the early 1990s, Cambodia's film infrastructure was non-existent and caused numerous logistical problems for the transport crew. To get to Siem Reap, the gateway to the Angkor Wat temples, meant hauling equipment on thirty trucks along roads littered with potholes and land mines. Escorted by the Royal Cambodian Army, and assisted by a minesweeper, the convoy often had to stop for hours while soldiers repaired the bridges ahead.

Each Cambodian worker was paid $500 per week – a year's salary for the natives scraping by on $2 a day – in what was seen by the

Cambodian government as an experimental glimpse into the boom future of their own, once great, film industry. Back in the 1960s, Cambodia had a small but vibrant national film industry, largely thanks to the patronage of their movie-crazy king, Norodom Sihanouk, who actually did become an acclaimed director. But Pol Pot single-handedly devastated the industry by executing most of the country's actors and directors. Conservationist Ashley Thompson of Cambodia's Apsara Temples Authority worked extremely closely with the production throughout the November 2000 shoot to ensure that no damage was done either to the locations or to the country's image. The $30,000 a day the production was charged for one week of photography went toward the conservational upkeep of the area, in particular the temple steps that, although well trodden for eight hundred years, haven't been able to cope with modern heavy footwear worn by tourists. "It's difficult to put into words the feeling you get when you walk through the temple causeway," says Simon an assignment, and determinedly power-glides her way through the morass of mud and water in her Land Rover, she's more than happy to be in Cambodia and learns many lessons besides being healed and given words of wisdom. She learns to listen to people, to be open to new things and to be led by the magic of

West. "The architecture is quite unbelievable just in terms of dimension and size, not to mention the sense of wonder that completely engulfs you. The bureaucracy and government channels we had to face were quite daunting but well worth the perseverance so we could capture the magical ambience of the place."

"It might have been a difficult undertaking but I think Angkor Wat was a vital choice of location for *Tomb Raider*," points out Angelina Jolie. "Lara has come here for the same reason that most people do – to replenish her spirit and seek refuge and peace. Although Lara is on life. For once she's not crashing through her high-powered existence but has stopped to smell the flowers along the way. Lara comes to Cambodia to find herself so she can embark on her quest with renewed zeal. The ultimate point of filming in Cambodia is that this is where her true strength lies waiting and when she finds it she becomes stronger than the others searching for the triangle puzzle pieces."

Aside from the Angkor Wat temples, *Tomb Raider* also filmed at other Cambodian locations. "Phnom Kulion was another striking place", says Nick Ray, writer of the *Lonely*

*Planet* guide to Cambodia and chosen by the production to help them cut through all the governmental red tape. "It's a very important Buddhist sanctuary because the Angkorian Empire based itself around the area when it first began in 802. King Shianouk was vital in securing this protected location because he was an enormous help in putting us in touch with the right people at the Ministry of Culture. You see, it wasn't just a case of getting permission to film somewhere as the authorities have to report back to the government and UNESCO. They are accountable as well and do not want any ill feeling or trouble caused."

It was Ray who recruited *Tomb Raider's* army of taxi drivers, guides, extras and interpreters. "We nicknamed then 'interrupters' as they did their own thing most of the time," he laughs. He continues, "And you know something? They all knew who Lara Croft was! The person we signed contracts with in Phnom Penh, his daughter was a Lara Croft fanatic and he told me she would never have forgiven him if he hadn't allowed us access. Such is the power of *Tomb Raider* even somewhere as remote as Cambodia."

"For so many reasons, *Tomb Raider* is destined to be movie of historical importance", remarks Jon Voight. "It's a magical mystery tour primarily filled with fun, excitement and fantasy. But on so many other levels it says a lot about the human condition and culture. Not just Icelandic or Cambodian culture but pop culture too. It is going to make audiences feel good and give them the chance to see things that are so special, precious and magnificent in today's world. "

He continues: "Tomb Raider is just like the films I took Angie to see when she was a little girl – ones she found inspirational and fired her imagination. Now she's the star of one of the greatest and I couldn't be any prouder of her than I am at this point in my life."

# The Cast

ANGELINA JOLIE . . . . . . . . . . . . . . . . . . . . Lara Croft
JON VOIGHT . . . . . . . . . . . . . . . . . . . . . Lord Croft
NOAH TAYLOR . . . . . . . . . . . . . . . . . . Bryce Turing
DANIEL CRAIG . . . . . . . . . . . . . . . . . . . . Alex West
IAIN GLEN . . . . . . . . . . . . . . . . . . Manfred Powell
JULIAN RHIND-TUTT . . . . . . . . . . . . . . . . . . Pimms
CHRISTOPHER BARRIE . . . . . . . . . . . . . . . . . Hillary

# Acknowledgements

Carlton Books and Alan Jones would like to thank the
following people for their assistance in producing this
book: Alex Bailey (principal photography) and Simon
Smith-Hutchon (additional photography); Susan D'Arcy
and Sarah Horsell at Pinewood and Paula Block and
Rita Kessler in the United States for their help in
putting everything together so swiftly; and all the
cast and crew of *Tomb Raider*, who made this book
possible.